To my family: thanks for believing in me.
To Londyn and Aden: always follow your dreams.
To my future and former students: don't ever be afraid to fix someone else's crown.

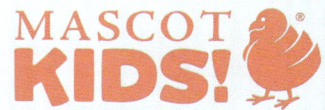

www.mascotbooks.com

## A CROOKED CROWN DAY

©2021 Brandie Hollingsworth. All Rights Reserved. No part of this publication may be reproduced, stored in a retrieval system or transmitted in any form by any means electronic, mechanical, or photocopying, recording or otherwise without the permission of the author.

For more information, please contact:
Mascot Books
620 Herndon Parkway, Suite 320
Herndon, VA 20170
info@mascotbooks.com

Library of Congress Control Number: 2020925765

CPSIA Code: PRT0221A
ISBN-13: 978-1-64543-768-0

Printed in the United States

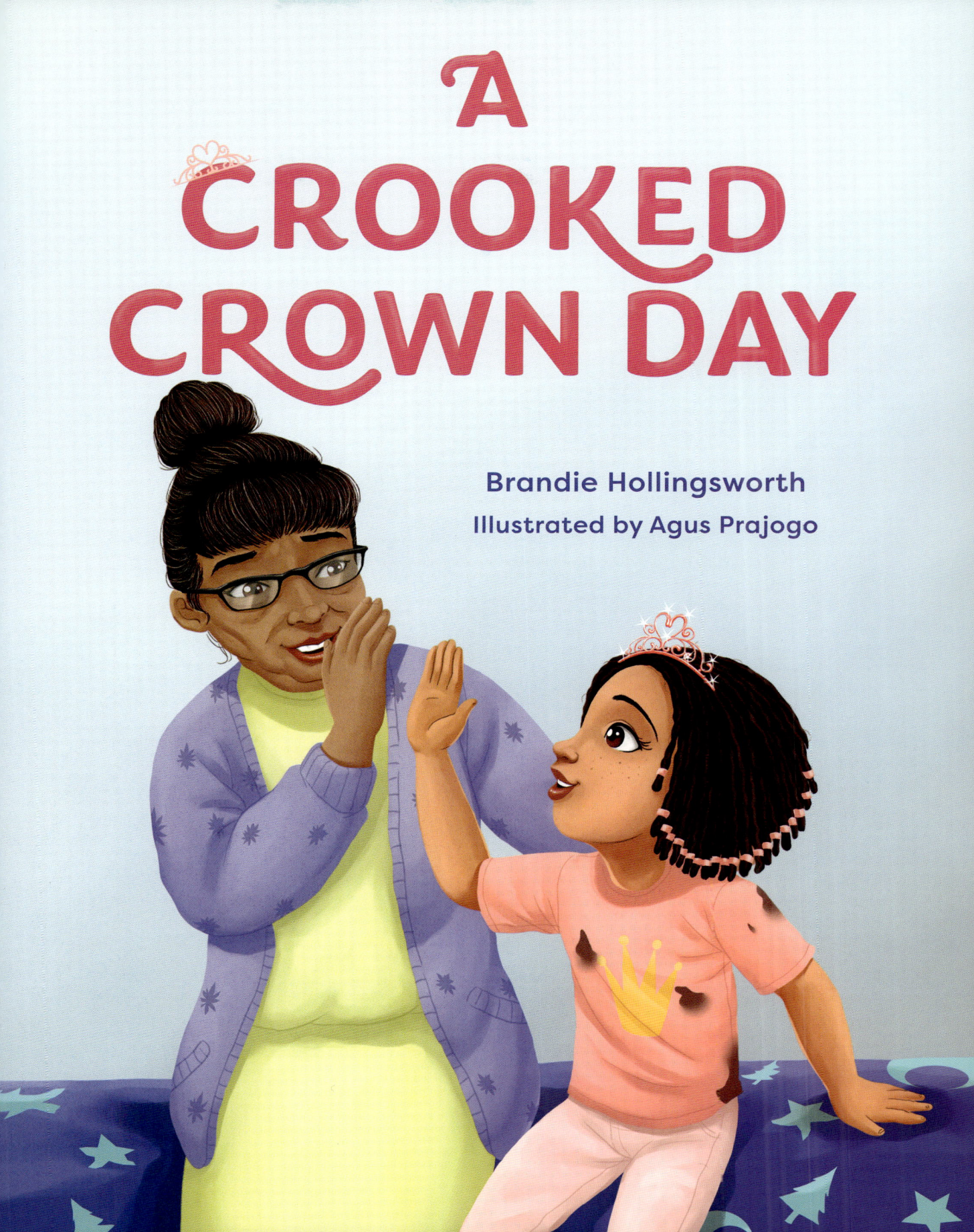

Lauren Londyn Renee Lee
always tried to let things be.
She usually wore a big, bright smile,
and was only sad once in a while.
But today was a different day, as you will see.
Today was the day things just wouldn't be.

As she waited for the school bus outside in the rain, her hair turned into an afro, and other students complained.

They arrived at school and she fell with a **thud!**
Her shoe flew off and she landed in the mud.
A crowd gathered around and began to laugh,
and no one stood up on her behalf.

The day carried on about the same.
Some kids ignored her and some called her names.

She went to gym class and the kids called her fat when she tried to do a cartwheel on top of the mat.

She forgot her math homework on the chair at home.
Then the teacher made her write in the back all alone.

And try as she may and try as she might,
by the time she got home, her crown
tilted down to the right.
Her head was bowed, her shoulders where low,
and to the ground her crown began to go.

Her grandmother caught it and placed it straight on her head.
She opened her mouth, and this is what she said . . .

"Put a smile on your face and dry your eyes. Tomorrow, let's give this week another try."

You have royal blood running through your veins,
and ancestors who walked this world with no shame.
Your head is filled with knowledge and dreams
that will come true,
but it's up to you to make it do what it do."

"So, fix your crown, little girl, and fly as high as you can.
And let no woman, girl, or man stop you from your plan.
This crown on your head tells your story,
so you keep it straight. It contains God's glory!"

So just like that, the crown was set straight, and Lauren Londyn Renee Lee couldn't wait. She gave her grandmother a high five and walked outside with her head held high.

As Lauren Londyn walked around her town,
she spotted a girl with a low-tilted crown.
She smiled at the girl as she stopped to say,
"Everybody has a crooked crown day!
Here, let me fix it so you can be on your way!"

We all wear an invisible crown,
but sometimes it gets tilted, and sometimes it falls down.
But, I will say: "It's okay,
to help another if you may,
fix their crooked crown!"

## ABOUT THE AUTHOR

By following her dreams of being a writer, Brandie Hollingsworth hopes to inspire someone else to follow their dreams. Brandie resides in Omaha, Nebraska, with her two children, Aden Stricklin and Londyn Lee. She is a dedicated eighth-grade English and language arts teacher. She hopes this book will help teach, inspire, and reinforce the importance of "fixing each other's crowns" for young girls everywhere.

beautifullycrookedcrown.com